FAST AND FURRY RACERS
The Silver Serpent Cup

Kane Miller
A DIVISION OF EDC PUBLISHING

Al McNasty

Max O'Moley

Baron Billy
Blackstripes

Roderick
Von Rooster

Stephanie Skedaddle

Ella Egghart

Shelley Bombard

Ollie Octolinni

Reverend Reginald
Spindly

Lord and Lady
Reynard

Heidi Highhorn

Theo Thunderfoot

Today the town of Furryville's a very noisy place,
Crammed with crowds of creatures getting ready for a race.

The air is filled with honking horns and engines revving up,
As racers take their places for . . .

THE SILVER SERPENT CUP!

From Furryville to Featherport a thousand miles away,
This pack of eager animals will get there in one day.

On the ground or in the air, floating or submersed,
There's just one rule: to win this race you have to get there FIRST!

All kinds of different vehicles are lined up at the start.
Some are sleek and shiny . . .

Everybody's ready,
so the race can now begin.

A siren sounds
and then
THEY'RE OFF
and may
the best
beast win!

and some
are not so
smart.

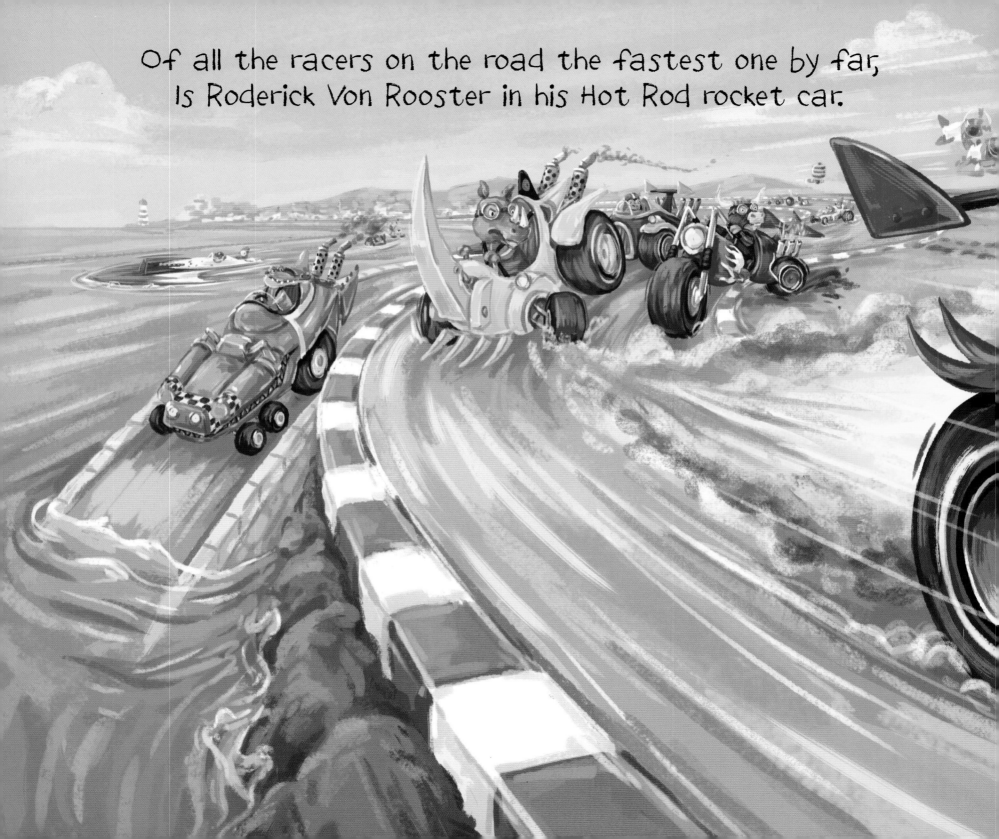

Of all the racers on the road the fastest one by far,
Is Roderick Von Rooster in his Hot Rod rocket car.

While all the other vehicles crowd together in a pack,
The Hot Rod fires its booster and then zooms off down the track.

Hurtling from the harbor and out across the bay,
Stephanie Skedaddle goes swiftly on her way.
Whooshing through the water in her sleek and stylish boat,
This seafaring sensation is the fastest thing afloat!

Creatures are competing UNDERNEATH the ocean too,
Where a shoal of submarines is bolting through the blue.

A shortcut through a shipwreck, carried out at breakneck speed,
Means that Ollie Octolinni has leapt into the lead.

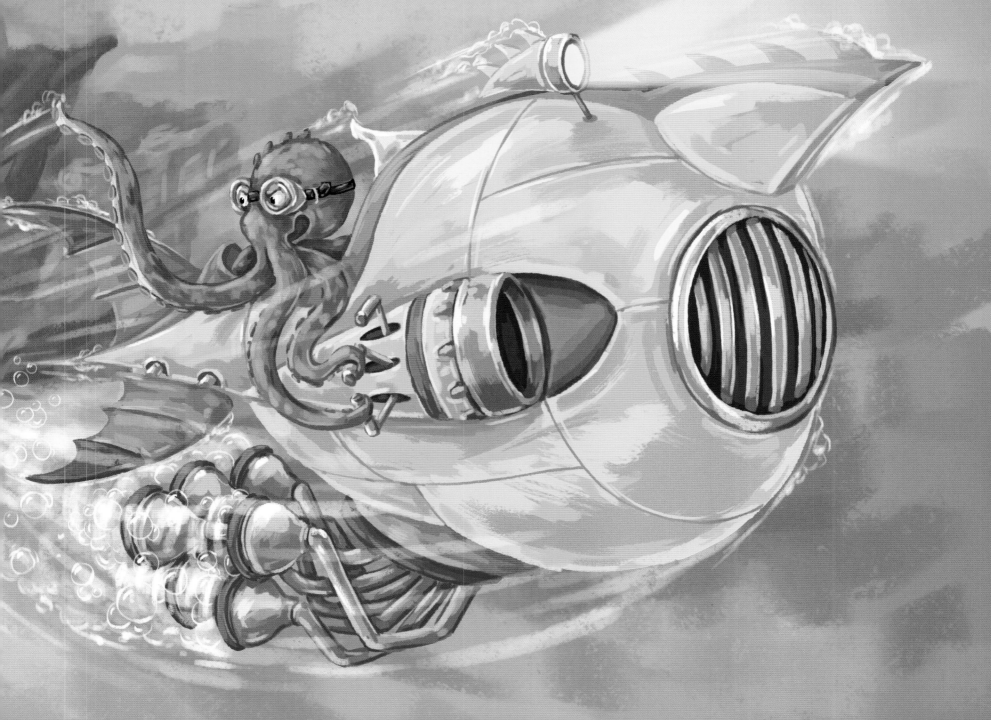

We're halfway through the race now and on dry land again,
Where Baron Billy Blackstripes is racing in a train!

Spotting Roderick's Hot Rod on the highway up ahead,
Billy roars right past him and takes the lead instead.

The competition's getting fierce and high up in the sky,
Ella Egghart's airplane has just come soaring by.

As Featherport comes into view she has a beaky grin.
Everyone's behind her, so surely she must win.

But if you think it's over, well you'll have to think again,
As rockets fly across the sky and BLOW UP Ella's plane.

There's rockets flying everywhere. They're hitting everyone.
And blowing up their vehicles until all of them are gone!

Who fired all those rockets? Well the villain isn't far,
It's awful Al McNasty in his armored aqua-car.

This ruthless, rotten reptile has a smug look on his face.
With all the other vehicles gone, he's bound to take first place.

Al's almost at the finish when he hears a rumbling sound,
And something big and pointy erupts OUT OF THE GROUND!
The rockets missed one racer who ran the race unseen,
And that was . . .

Max O'Moley in his tunneling machine!

Max comes UP THROUGH the finish line to thunderous applause,
And swiftly snatches victory from Al's astonished jaws.
Of all the ways to win the race, Al's had to be the worst,
So everyone's delighted that Max has come in first!

Tonight the town of Featherport's a very noisy place,
As everybody celebrates a most momentous race.
And all the other animals whose vehicles were blown up,
Cheer for Max, the winner of . . .

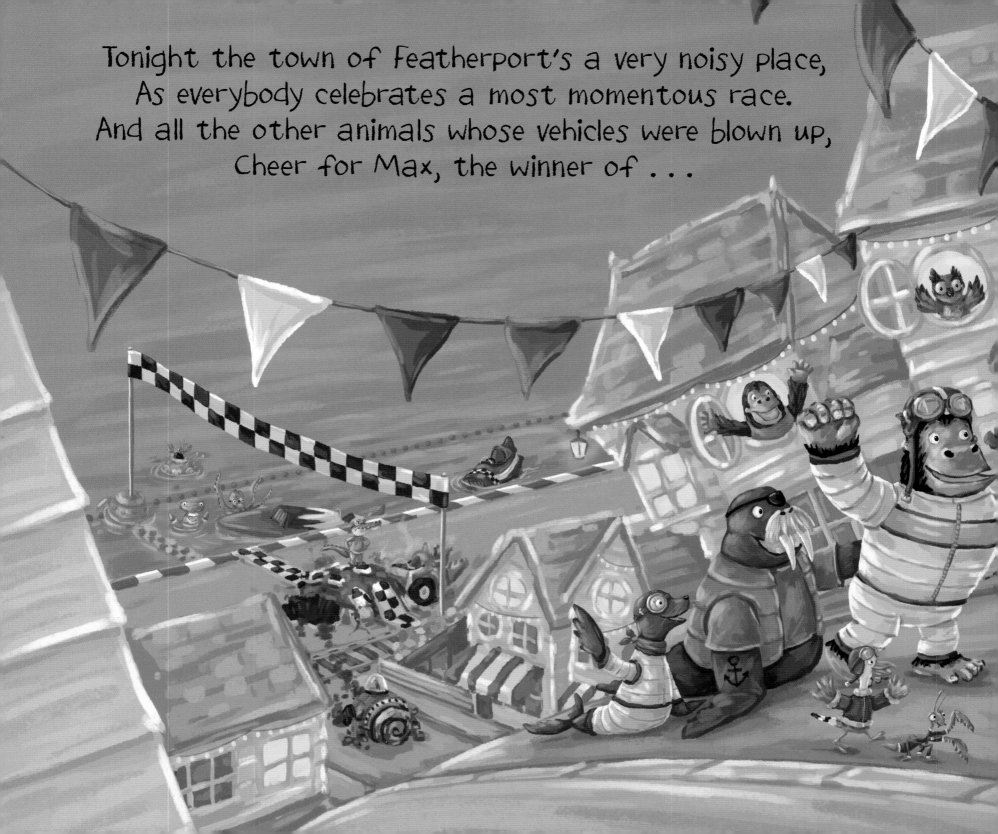

For the children of Asfordby Captain's Close Primary School. J.E.
For Theodore xx. E.E

First American Edition 2017
Kane Miller, A Division of EDC Publishing

Text © Jonathan Emmett, 2015
Illustrations © Ed Eaves, 2015

Fast and Furry Racers was originally published in English in 2014. This edition is published by arrangement with Oxford University Press.

For information contact:
Kane Miller, A Division of EDC Publishing
PO Box 470663
Tulsa, OK 74147-0663
www.kanemiller.com
www.edcpub.com
www.usbornebooksandmore.com

Library of Congress Control Number: 2016934244

Printed in China
1 2 3 4 5 6 7 8 9 10

ISBN: 978-1-61067-544-4

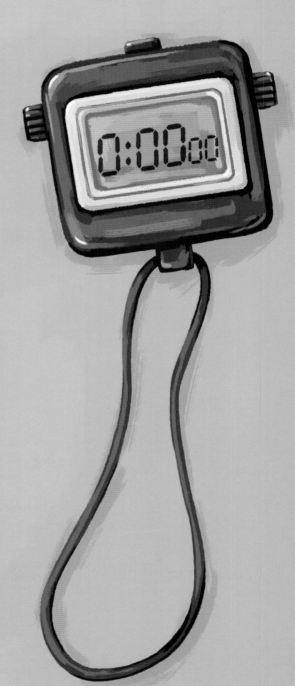

Bruce and Barney Battenberg

Burt Bourguignon

Hank "The Hammer" Chompski

Bucky Hopkins

Doctor Waldo Snapper

Sir Hugo Hefflington

Salvador Squawky

Posy Pinkerton

Otto Von Skirmish

Sergeant Boris Blastovich

Gertrude Kerfuffle

Bess and Bonnie Bumblebutt